THE
EASY CLASSICS
EPIC COLLECTION

Published by Sweet Cherry Publishing Limited
Unit 36, Vulcan House,
Vulcan Road,
Leicester, LE5 3EF
United Kingdom

First published in the UK in 2021
2021 edition

2 4 6 8 10 9 7 5 3 1

ISBN: 978-1-78226-783-6

The Easy Classics Epic Collection: Three Sisters

Based on the original story by Anton Chekhov,
adapted by Gemma Barder.

Cover design by Helen Panayi and Dominika Plocka
Illustrations by Helen Panayi

Lexile® code numerical measure L = Lexile® 700L

www.sweetcherrypublishing.com

Printed and bound in Turkey
T.IO006

THREE SISTERS

Anton Chekhov

Sweet Cherry

The Prozorovs

Olga Prozorov
Sister

Masha Prozorov
Sister

Irina Prozorov
Sister

Andrey Prozorov
Brother

Natasha Prozorov
Andrey's wife

Fyodor Kulygin
Masha's husband

Anfisa
The Prozorovs' maid

THE BATTALION

Alexander Vershinin

Baron Tuzenbakh

Vasily Solyony

Doctor Chebutykin

PART ONE

Chapter One

Olga, Masha and Irina Prozorov were sisters. They lived in a beautiful house in a small town with their brother, Andrey. The town was a day's carriage ride from Moscow, but the sisters often felt it was the other side of the world.

Although the town was peaceful and friendly, it couldn't compare to the busy streets, museums and theatres in Moscow. The Prozorov family had moved from Moscow many years ago when their father had been made general of the battalion stationed in the town. Their mother passed away not long after, and their father followed years later. The sisters and their young brother inherited the house.

On this particular day, the sisters were feeling a mixture of happiness and sadness. It was Irina's twentieth birthday, but it was also the anniversary of their father's death.

'I cannot believe it has been a whole year,' Olga sighed. She was the eldest of the sisters by eight years. After their parents died, she became like a mother to her younger siblings. Olga rested her hands on a pile of essays she had been marking. 'It was snowing on the day of father's funeral, and we were all so dreadfully sad.'

Olga had worked at the local school for a few years. She had been made deputy headmistress and all the sisters said how proud their father would have been of her.

'But today we shall feel happy,' Olga continued, standing up from her desk and stretching. 'It is your birthday, Irina! If only Andrey would stop playing his violin and come and join us. Our guests will be arriving soon.'

Irina smiled. She had been standing looking out of the window dreamily, remembering the life they once had when their parents were alive.

At that moment, Anfisa, their elderly maid, hobbled into the room.

She was carrying a cake so large she could barely see over the top of it.

'Oh, Irina, your birthday cake!' said Olga, taking the cake from Anfisa. 'Anfisa, you have done it again. It looks delicious.' The old lady smiled a toothless grin, waved her hand and hobbled back towards the kitchen.

'Masha, take a look at the cake!' Olga called over to her sister. Masha was lying on a sofa on the other side of their large sitting room. Her nose was pressed firmly into one of their father's old books.

'I can see it from here,' Masha said, giving a small smile. 'It looks beautiful, Irina.' Masha returned to her book and Olga sighed.

Masha was the only one of the Prozorov sisters who was married. When she was eighteen, Masha had believed her husband, Fyodor, was a clever man with great ambition. He was a schoolteacher like Olga, but Masha had been certain he was destined for greater things. As the years had passed, however, Masha had begun to realise that she was far more intelligent than her husband. He was kind, but would never be anything more than he already was.

The pain of realising she was married to a man she did not really love or admire had made Masha tired and miserable. Although she was only twenty-three, she felt years older.

Olga ignored her sister's lack of interest and turned back to Irina. 'What is your birthday wish, Irina?' she said, grasping her sister's hands.

Irina's blue eyes sparkled. She was the youngest of the sisters and hoped for a happy life ahead of her. 'I wish to return to Moscow!' Irina replied, happily.

Olga laughed. 'Oh, Moscow! That is a splendid wish. We were all so happy there with Mother and Father. Yes, we shall go home to Moscow.'

Although Irina knew Olga was only dreaming, she liked to pretend it was true.

Masha smiled at her sisters sadly. She loved their optimism and cheerfulness, but inside she felt trapped. She knew that even if her sisters did move back to Moscow one day, she would have to stay with her husband.

Chapter Two

Many of the officers in General Prozorov's battalion had grown fond of the Prozorov family. The general had been a good man and a fair leader, and the officers vowed they would watch over the family after he died. In fact, three of their father's old friends were joining the Prozorovs to celebrate Irina's birthday.

Baron Tuzenbakh was a little older than the sisters. He came from an important family and, although he wasn't as handsome as some of the other officers, he always had something interesting to talk about.

Doctor Chebutykin was the battalion's doctor. He had been a good friend of General Prozorov and his wife. Although the Doctor was getting old, he stayed on in the army as well as keeping a close eye on the Prozorov children.

Vasily Solyony was a stern gentleman with dark hair and black eyes. He had greatly admired General Prozorov. Solyony said things in a loud, brash voice and, although the sisters found him slightly unnerving to be around, they always invited him to gatherings as he was good friends with the Baron.

The three officers entered the sitting room with armfuls of presents. They happily greeted each sister, and even Masha got up from the sofa to say hello.

She kissed the Doctor warmly on each cheek and guided him to a comfortable chair.

'I hope you do not mind, Olga,' said the Baron. 'I have invited our new lieutenant to join us.'

The sisters exchanged glances. It was not often that they met new people in this small town, so it was always exciting when they did.

'May I introduce Alexander Vershinin,' the Baron said. 'Although, I believe you have met already.'

Alexander Vershinin looked as though he was in his mid-thirties, and was tall with a handsome, kind face.

'I'm sorry, Lieutenant,' said Olga, smiling. 'I'm afraid I don't remember you.'

Alexander smiled back. 'We were all much younger then. Your father was the general of my battalion in Moscow.'

'Moscow!' Irina gasped. 'You are from Moscow?'

'Yes,' replied Alexander. 'I lived not far from you. I was very sad to hear of General Prozorov's death.'

A moment of silence fell in the sitting room before Solyony could be heard loudly asking for a drink and enquiring when lunch would be served. Solyony felt awkward in such emotional moments and often filled them with his voice. Olga, Irina and the Baron went to talk to him.

'I remember you,' Alexander said, looking at Masha. Masha stared into his deep brown eyes.

'Yes, I do too,' she said. 'I think Olga and I had a nickname for you. We called you the Lovesick Major!'

Alexander laughed. 'Oh yes! You teased me about being in love with a local girl.'

Masha found herself laughing too. She realised it was the first time she had laughed for days.

'Did you marry the girl?' Masha asked.

Alexander stopped laughing and his face became serious. 'Ah, no,' he said. 'But I am married now. I have two beautiful little girls.'

Masha thought that this should be something any husband and father would be pleased to talk about. But Alexander looked almost sad.

CHAPTER THREE

Anfisa popped her head into the sitting room to announce that lunch was ready. The guests chatted happily as they made their way towards the dining room. They could hear the sound of a violin being played.

'That is just Andrey,' Olga said, gesturing to a door that led to her brother's music room. 'He is rather talented, but he gets so carried away by his music that he forgets the time!' Olga knocked on the door and the music stopped.

A young man with messy hair poked his head out of the room. He looked slightly startled to see the group in the hallway. 'Oh! Is it that time already?' Andrey said as he stepped out to meet the group, his violin and bow still in his hand.

'Forgive me, Irina! I'll be right there.'

Andrey dashed back into his music room to fetch his jacket and smooth his hair.

'Your brother was very little when I last saw him,' Alexander said as he took a seat next to Masha at the long dining table. 'I never thought he would turn into a musician.'

Suddenly, Fyodor burst into the room. 'I am sorry I could not come sooner!' he chuckled. 'You would think I was in high demand, but I simply forgot the time!'

The little balloon of happiness Masha had been feeling since she started talking to Alexander seemed to burst as soon as her husband entered the room.

'Where is my darling wife? Ah! There you are!' he laughed as he sat on the other side of Masha and was introduced to Alexander. Masha stiffened as Fyodor kissed her cheek.

Then the final guest at the party arrived, peeking her head around the dining room door as though she were uncertain whether she should be there or not. Natasha was a young woman from town. It was clear she wasn't used to being in such a grand house or having lunch with officers.

Natasha had been invited by Andrey. They had met in town not long after General Prozorov had passed away. Andrey had been feeling particularly sad that day, and Natasha had cheered him up. He had loved her ever since.

Olga rose from her seat to greet her. 'Natasha, how lovely to see you,' Olga said, ushering her towards the table. 'That's an … original colour dress you have on today.'

Natasha's face flushed red. She looked down at her bright green dress with its frilled neckline. 'Is it? I thought it would be right for a luncheon,' she said, flustered.

Olga looked her up and down. 'Well, it's perfectly fine for today.'

Natasha slid into the remaining empty seat next to Andrey. She could not bring herself to talk to him, feeling so ashamed by her choice of dress. She looked around at the sisters, who were all wearing fine, pale muslin dresses with high necks and faint patterns. She stood out like a cheap Christmas decoration in a pile of feathers.

CHAPTER FOUR

As Anfisa slowly served the lunch to the guests, the Baron said, 'Well now! What shall we discuss over this fine meal?'

'I would like to say how happy I am to be with you all after such a long time,' said Alexander, raising his glass. 'I could not imagine it five years ago.'

The Baron slapped his hand on the table. 'That's it! The Lieutenant could not imagine his life leading to this moment five years ago. Let us discuss where we would like our lives to be in five years' time.'

The group fell silent as they ate and thought about their answers. Irina and Olga went first. They declared that they would like to

be back in Moscow, in their old house, surrounded by friends just as lovely as the ones they had here.

The Doctor chuckled that he would like to still be alive, and the Baron declared that whatever he

had in five years' time would be a result of the work he did now.

Fyodor declared that he wished to be exactly as he was now in five years' time. This made Masha's heart sink. She felt she would be even more unhappy if nothing changed in her life in five years, although she didn't say it out loud.

Solyony refused to answer; to him the discussion was silly and pointless.

Then, Alexander stood up. 'I cannot say what will happen in the next few years, but I have learnt one thing.' He glanced at

Masha, then back to the room. 'We must try to live as if the past were a rehearsal for our lives now. To learn from our mistakes and try not to make them again.' The dining room fell silent. Alexander spoke in such a way that even Solyony, who rarely valued other people's opinions, was forced to listen.

'As some of you know, my wife is unwell. But I have two lovely daughters whom I would not change. I have much I could complain about, but much to be happy about too. I say, "Happy

Birthday" to Irina, and thank you all for having me today.'

To that, the party all cheered 'Happy Birthday' in unison and clinked their glasses together happily.

As the lunch continued, Andrey noticed that Natasha was not her usual self. When they were alone together, Natasha was much more confident, constantly chatting to Andrey. But here she rarely spoke. Andrey knew his sisters did not think she was good enough for him. Natasha was not from a wealthy family and she didn't know the proper way to dress for formal occasions. But none of that mattered to Andrey. To him she was perfect. Natasha was full of life and Andrey was certain she would make him happy for the rest of his days.

'Natasha, what is the matter?' Andrey asked quietly, so as not to draw the attention of the other guests.

Natasha began to sniffle. 'It is your sisters,' she said, 'and their friends. The Baron, that doctor, they all look down on me. They laugh at me!'

Andrey gently took Natasha by the arm and led her out of the dining room. They sat together on a small balcony overlooking the gardens. 'My dear, I am sure what you say is not true.'

'It is!' said Natasha, forcefully. Now they were alone, her confidence returned. When it was just herself and Andrey, Natasha felt as though they were equals. 'You let them boss

you about and soon they will tell
you not to see me!'

Andrey shook his head. He
fumbled in the pockets of his jacket
and pulled out a beautiful diamond
ring. It glittered in the afternoon
sun. 'No one can tell me what to
do,' he said, seriously. 'This ring
was my mother's. I would like it
to be yours. Will you marry me,
Natasha?'

Natasha stared at
the ring. She knew
that as Andrey's wife
she would be equal to
his sisters. She would

be wealthy and live in a big house.
She took the ring and placed it on
her finger. 'Yes!' she replied.

PART TWO

CHAPTER ONE

Two years passed. Andrey and Natasha were married and Natasha moved into the house with Andrey and his sisters. Soon, they had a baby boy named Bobik. Natasha doted on the little boy and cared about his needs above all else.

One evening, as they sat in the sitting room watching the sun go down and sipping tea, Natasha sighed. Andrey had noticed that his wife sighed a lot recently.

Usually, she sighed before she started to complain about something. This evening was no exception.

'Another beautiful day and still our little Bobik's room is cold,' she said. 'I don't think it's fair that Irina's room is always full of sunlight and warmth when my little baby is shivering in his cot.'

Andrey rubbed his forehead. Since Natasha had moved into the Prozorov house, she had started to make little changes here and there. The first was to insist that she and Andrey took his parents' old room, which was by far the largest in the entire house. Before then, no one had wanted to move General Prozorov's belongings. Now the room looked completely different.

Natasha had taken charge of Anfisa, too, bossing her about far more than Olga or Irina ever would. Now she wanted Irina to move out of her bedroom to make way for baby Bobik.

'My dear,' said Andrey, wearily. 'May I remind you that this house belongs to Olga and Irina, too. In fact, it belongs to Masha as well.'

Natasha stood up, annoyed. 'Olga and Irina do not have babies to think of, and Masha doesn't live here!' Then she added with a huff: 'Although she is here so often you would think that she did.'

Anfisa entered the room before Andrey could answer. She was carrying a thick file of papers. 'These were delivered for you, sir,' she said, plopping the file down on Andrey's desk. The desk used to be Olga's for marking her pupils' essays, until Natasha suggested it would be better if Olga did that in her room.

'More work from the district council,' Andrey sighed. He glanced longingly at his violin. It was propped in a corner of the living room collecting dust. When Bobik was born, Natasha suggested that working at the council would be a far more respectable job for a father than playing the violin. She looked at the file happily.

'Good,' she said. 'It must mean they can't do without you! Now, I'm going to see if darling Bobik has woken from his nap.'

Andrey opened up the file and flipped through it, uninterested. He found his job boring. He still loved Natasha very much, and being a father was everything he could have wished for, but he missed his violin.

Anfisa shuffled back into the room with a cup of tea and Andrey's favourite biscuits on a tray.

'Thank you,' he said, getting up and popping the file under his arm. 'I will have it in my music room – I mean my study.'

Chapter Two

Olga and Irina were excited. Each year a group of musicians visited their little town, and each year they were invited to the Prozorovs' house to put on a private performance.

As soon as Olga returned
from school, the sisters set about
turning the sitting room into a
miniature concert hall. They were
so busy arranging the chairs and
discussing where each musician
should sit that they did not see
Masha and Alexander arrive.

'Look at my sisters!' said Masha, happily. 'This is one of their favourite days of the year. It reminds them of Moscow. We had concerts like this all the time, do you remember?'

Alexander nodded. 'I do. Your mother enjoyed them very much.'

Over the past two years, Masha and Alexander had become good friends. They liked the same books and artists, and enjoyed walking in the park together. After a while, Alexander had told Masha all about his wife and how they often argued.

Masha found that she enjoyed spending time with Alexander far more than with her husband, Fyodor. They had more in common, and Alexander could make her laugh – something Fyodor had never been able to do.

'Mother and Father both liked music,' Masha said. 'It was like they

were meant to be together, they
had so much in common.'

'As do we,' said Alexander quietly.
Then, after a long pause, he said:
'Oh Masha, you must know that
I am in love with you.'

Masha's heart soared. She
had hardly dared to hope that
Alexander might be in love
with her as she was with him.
Before Masha could
reply, they were
interrupted by
Baron Tuzenbakh
who entered the
sitting room

clapping happily. 'What a perfect arrangement!' he cried.

'Yes,' said Masha, joining her sisters. 'You've done a wonderful job. Shall we have some tea while we wait for the guests to arrive?'

The group sat happily on the sofas that had been pushed back against a far wall. Anfisa brought tea and cake, which Olga served. She insisted that Anfisa stay a while and have tea with them. The old maid had been with the Prozorov family for nearly twenty years, and had known the sisters as babies. They saw her as a family friend and tried not to give her too much to do in her old age – unlike Natasha.

'Oh, if only every day could be like this!' said Irina, passing a slice of cake to the Baron.

'What can I do to make it so?' he said. 'I will ask a hundred musicians to come and perform if it will make you happy!'

Everyone laughed at the Baron. Over the years he had grown to love Irina very much, and he wasn't shy about letting her, or anyone, know it.

'I do not need a hundred musicians,' Irina said, smiling. 'If you could help my poor brother, that would make me happy. Masha, did you know he has been gambling again?'

Masha put down her tea. She was not surprised that Andrey

had been gambling. Although he never admitted it, she knew he was unhappy.

'Should we tell Natasha?' asked Olga.

Masha shook her head. 'If it is not to do with baby Bobik, she is not interested.'

An awkward silence fell across the party as they contemplated Natasha and Andrey. It was interrupted by Natasha herself, who flew angrily into the room.

'This note has arrived for Lieutenant Vershinin,' she said. 'I had to answer the door *myself*, and now I see why!' Natasha glared at Anfisa. 'It is *your* job to answer the door. We do not pay you to sit and have tea and cake, you lazy old woman!'

Olga came to Anfisa's side as the maid struggled to her feet and apologised.

'You have nothing to apologise for,' Olga said. 'Natasha, this woman has lived in this house and been part of this family longer than you. You will treat her with respect.'

The argument distracted Masha from Alexander. He was reading the note Natasha had handed him, and his face was turning pale. 'It is my wife,' he said. 'She has left the children on their own again. I must go to them.'

Masha watched unhappily as Alexander left the room. She wished she could help him. But, above all, she wished she could be married to him herself.

Chapter Three

Later that evening, the musicians arrived and began to set up their instruments in the sitting room. Irina fluttered around them, making sure they had everything they needed.

Solyony and Doctor Chebutykin had joined the party, and even Andrey had been glad of the excuse to leave his work. Masha watched the door to see if Alexander would return.

Olga tried to convince Anfisa to stay for the concert, but the old woman was tired and went to bed. If Natasha were there, instead of upstairs tending to Bobik, she would have insisted that Anfisa stay to serve wine to their guests. Instead, Olga brought apple juice around to the guests herself.

Soon it was time for the concert to begin. The music started softly, with beautiful Russian folk songs.

When their mother and father's favourite tune began, the sisters smiled at one another, and at Andrey. However, their memories of happier times were soon shattered.

'Stop! This must stop!'

It was Natasha who spoke. She was standing in the doorway, her face flushed with anger. The musicians stopped playing and looked to Irina and Olga, confused.

'The music is too loud. Little Bobik cannot sleep, and he has a terrible temperature,' Natasha said. 'I am afraid the concert has to end. Now.'

Masha stood up. 'Bobik was fine when I played with him this afternoon,' she said.

Natasha folded her arms. 'Perhaps it was you who passed something on to him!'

Andrey lay a hand on his sister's arm to stop her from saying anything back to his wife. 'Perhaps, if the child is poorly, we should stop the concert,' he said.

Irina and Olga looked so disappointed, Masha thought they may cry.

The Doctor offered to take a look at Bobik, but Natasha shooed him away. 'I am perfectly capable of looking after him myself. He just needs to sleep.'

As the musicians packed up their instruments, Olga apologised. Irina fled to her room in tears and the officers made their way out of the room.

'Are you sure you don't want me to stay?' Doctor Chebutykin asked Andrey, who shook his head.

'In that case, I know of a card game going on not too far from here. Would you like to join?'

Andrey looked around the sitting room to make sure his wife had left. If she saw him, she was sure to insist that he stay and helped her with Bobik. Certain the coast was clear, he followed the doctor out into the evening air.

The sitting room felt cold and empty. Irina had spent the last hour in her room, snivelling. When she came back downstairs,

all the guests had left and Olga
had gone to bed. The room had
not been put back to normal and
Irina stared at the makeshift
concert hall miserably.

'Irina?' said a voice. It was
Solyony. 'I am sorry to disturb you.'

'I thought everyone had left,'
Irina said, a little surprised to see
him there.

'I waited until everyone had
gone. I wanted to speak to you in
private,' Solyony said. He cleared
his throat and straightened the tie
on his uniform. 'Irina, I believe you
and I should be married.'

Irina was shocked. She had not thought Solyony liked her, let alone liked her enough to be his wife.

'I … I don't understand,' Irina said.

Solyony nodded. 'I know. It might seem like an odd thing to say. I do not pay calls on you or ask you to dance. I think all that is a waste of time. If you like someone you should just come out and say it. And please believe me when I say

I love you most fiercely. I would kill any man who stood in the way of our marriage.'

Irina covered her face with her hands. A proposal was the last thing she had imagined would happen today. A proposal from Solyony was even more unexpected.

'I … I can't think right now,' Irina said. She felt tears sting in the back of her eyes. 'Please leave, Solyony. Please.' As she said this, she realised that

she could never accept him as her husband.

Solyony gave Irina a polite bow, his face showing no emotion. Then he left the room as though being dismissed by his general, rather than the love of his life.

'Oh! I though everyone had left!' Natasha said. She was standing in her nightgown in the doorway, looking embarrassed as Solyony passed her. 'I am glad you are awake, Irina. I need to discuss something with you.'

Irina looked at her sister-in-law with hatred. Natasha had ruined one of the only evenings in the whole year that made her life in this small town happy.

'I wondered if you would swap rooms with little Bobik,' Natasha said. 'Or better still, you could move into Olga's room with her? I fear that Bobik is always catching a cold, and your room is always so warm.'

As much as Irina disliked Natasha, she loved her nephew. Silently, Irina nodded, and left the room.

PART THREE

CHAPTER ONE

All thoughts of the concert were forgotten when a terrible fire swept through the town a few weeks later. The flames spread quickly, reaching where the army was stationed. On the night of the blaze, Olga, Irina and Andrey opened up the Prozorov house to the officers who had lost their quarters to the fire.

Olga and Irina's room was turned into a temporary dormitory. The Baron dozed on an armchair by the fire while Olga, Masha and Irina folded blankets with Anfisa, to be given out around the town. Fyodor was slumped by the doorway. He had been helping to evacuate the school in case the fire reached it, and had fallen asleep, exhausted.

'What a terrible night!' cried Irina.

'Is it night or morning?' said Olga. 'I am so tired I can't tell! Masha, are the Vershinins settled?'

Masha nodded. Alexander's home had been destroyed by the fire and his family were now in one of their guest bedrooms.

'Anfisa, I need you in the kitchen,' snapped Natasha. The old woman, exhausted by the late hour, moved slowly across the room. When she had left, Natasha said: 'It is time we got rid of that woman.'

Olga nearly dropped the blanket she was carrying. 'That is out of the question!' she said.

Natasha sighed. 'She is no use to us anymore. I cannot have useless people cluttering up the house.'

Olga was so tired, and so angry, that she nearly burst into tears. She did not have the strength to argue.

'You must understand, Olga,' Natasha said, as though she were talking to Bobik rather than her sister-in-law. 'You are at the school all day, working. I am at home. I must take charge of the house and how it is run.'

Before Olga could reply, Doctor Chebutykin stumbled into the room. 'Lost! All is lost!' he cried, before flopping onto Olga's bed. It was clear that the Doctor was exhausted after the long night. He didn't look like he was feeling well.

'Has your house been lost, Doctor?' asked Irina, concerned. 'You are welcome to stay here.'

The Doctor sat up unsteadily and knocked over a small clock that always sat by Olga's bedside.

The noise woke the Baron and Fyodor from their slumber.

'Your mother's clock!' cried the Doctor. He sighed and rubbed his eyes. 'Your mother thought I was a good doctor. I *was* a good doctor. Now I am no use to anyone. I am far too old.'

Fyodor got to his feet. It was time for the Doctor to go to sleep. 'Come, Doctor,' he said, kindly. 'We have a room at our house you may stay in.'

The Doctor patted Fyodor's arm. 'You are a dear man. I do not know why your wife prefers Vershinin's company to yours!'

For a moment, the room went completely still. Although they never spoke of it, the sisters knew that Masha and Alexander were very much in love with each other. Deep down Fyodor knew it, too. However, he smiled at the Doctor and took a deep breath. 'I think this exhausting night must have gone to your head!' he said, waving off the comment.

'Let us get you to bed.'

CHAPTER TWO

The night of the fire dragged on. With each new arrival at the Prozorovs' house came a new story. The school building had not burnt down, but the council offices were destroyed. The army barracks were gone, and the soldiers were scattered with different families around the town.

Although there was not much more the sisters could do, they could not seem to sleep. Masha's eyes brightened when Alexander knocked and entered Olga and Irina's room. 'I hoped you would be awake,' he said.

'Come in, Lieutenant,' said Olga. 'Our room is open to all, as you can see!' Olga gestured to the corner where the Baron still slept, his uniform and face stained with soot.

Alexander made his way to Masha. She wished she could hold his hand and rest her head against his shoulder. 'Are your family settled?' she asked him.

Alexander nodded. 'My wife does not understand what is happening,' he said, sadly. 'But she is asleep now, with the girls either side of her.'

Masha looked down, suddenly feeling very guilty. When she was with Alexander, she tried to forget that he had a family. 'They must feel safe with her,' she said.

'I do not think they do,' Alexander replied. 'Sometimes she forgets about them and wanders out of the house. Once she forgot to dress them and they stayed in their nightclothes all day long.'

Masha felt badly for Alexander's wife. She was not well, and it was not her fault that she acted the way she did. She took Alexander's hand and held it for a moment.

'Masha, it is time to go home,' Fyodor said. After settling the Doctor at their house, he had come back to fetch Masha.

Alexander nodded a silent goodbye to Masha and left the room to return to his wife and children.

'You are such a caring person, Masha,' said Fyodor. 'Lieutenant Vershinin has a lot to deal with. It is nice that he has you as his friend.'

Masha could not stand to hear her husband talk in such a kind way about her. She knew that it was unfair to him that she had fallen in love with someone else. She was sure Fyodor knew that she was in love with Vershinin, but all he did was praise her.

'I am so lucky, don't you think, Irina? Olga?' Fyodor pushed his glasses up his nose a little. Olga and Irina looked at each other, not knowing how to answer. 'I cannot begin to tell you how much I love you, Masha.'

Each of Fyodor's words hit Masha like a brick. She felt smothered, unhappy and guilty. The trauma of the evening and the late hour bubbled up inside her. 'But I am so bored!' she shouted. 'I am so unhappy!'

Fyodor looked at his wife in shock. When he did not speak, Olga rushed

to his side. 'It has been a long night,' she said, kindly. 'Masha is exhausted. Try not to pay too much attention to what she says.'

Fyodor nodded. He looked at his wife who was now weeping into her hands.

'Maybe Masha could sleep here tonight?' suggested Irina. 'We can put a bed in our room. It will be just like when we were young.'

Fyodor nodded. 'Yes,' he said, quietly backing out of the room. 'Perhaps you are right.'

CHAPTER THREE

Carrying pillows and blankets for Masha's bed, Irina wearily climbed back up the steps to the room she shared with Olga. She felt so tired she could have laid on the stairs and fallen asleep right there.

'May I help you?' the Baron said. 'I was just leaving to see if I could be of any further help in the town.'

Irina smiled and handed him the blankets. 'Thank you,' she said. 'Anfisa tells me the fire is almost out.'

The Baron nodded. 'That is good. Although, without our barracks, I don't know how long the battalion will be able to stay in town. We cannot sleep on people's floors forever.'

Irina was shocked. The officers in the battalion were their oldest friends. If they left, the town would feel so empty.

'Irina, I wanted to talk to you alone and now seems like a good time,' said the Baron, putting down the blankets and holding Irina's hand. 'You must know that I am in love with you. I first felt it on your twentieth birthday. You were so happy and carefree back then.'

Irina swallowed. The Baron had never disguised the fact that he loved her, but now his face was serious. She knew what he was about to ask her.

'I am going to quit the army and return to my family in Moscow. My house is large, and I believe you would be happy there,' the Baron said. On hearing the word 'Moscow' Irina's face broke into a smile. 'Irina, I am asking you to be my wife.'

'Thank you, Baron,' Irina said politely. This was not her first proposal – although it was the first one she thought she might accept. She did not think that she was in love with the Baron, but she did like him very much. He was a kind man, and he was offering to take her back to Moscow. Her head ached with confusion. 'It is far too late, and I am far too tired, to give you an answer now. But I will think about it. I promise.' Irina squeezed the Baron's hand and smiled.

The Baron grinned back. He helped Irina to make Masha's bed in her room, then left. At last the sisters were alone.

'What a night,' Olga said, falling heavily on her bed. She felt old and tired.

After a moment's silence, Irina said: 'The Baron proposed.' Olga sat up straight in shock, and Masha jumped off her bed.

'What answer did you give him?' Masha asked.

'I told him I would think about it,' replied Irina.

The three sisters perched on Olga's bed, with Irina sat in the middle. Olga and Masha each took one of her hands.

'I think you should say yes,' said Olga. 'He loves you very much, he is a good man and he comes from a good family.'

'But do you love him?' asked Masha. 'You must be sure you love him before you say yes.'

Irina shook her head slightly, not knowing how to answer Masha's question. She did not

think she knew
what love was.

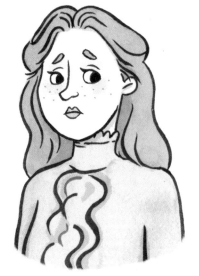

'I always thought
we would return to
Moscow one day,
and that I would
meet my true love there,' Irina
said, laughing at the idea.

'Love is not the most important
thing in a marriage,' said Olga.
'You must want the same things
and be able to take care of one
another. If I had been proposed
to and had a husband, I would
want him to be a good man like the
Baron. I would learn to love him.'

But Masha disagreed.

'Oh, Olga! How can you say that? You have never married, so you do not know how awful it is to be married to a man you do not love!'

Olga stood up and walked away from her sisters. Although Masha's words were true, it still upset her to be reminded that she was not married.

'But I know,' said Masha, sadly. She took a deep breath and looked at her sisters. She had never said the words out loud before now. 'I know because I do not love Fyodor. I love Alexander.'

PART
FOUR

Chapter One

Sun shone through the trees leaving dappled sunlight on the lawn outside the Prozorov house. The fire that had torn through the town a month ago seemed like a distant memory. People were starting to rebuild their homes, but as the Baron had predicted, the battalion were preparing to leave town. Olga was going to miss her friends dearly, especially as Irina was also about to leave –

she was to marry the Baron and move to Moscow.

Irina had thought about the Baron's proposal for days. In the end, she agreed with Olga that the Baron was a kind man who would look after her. She was certain that, over time, her love for him would grow, and the two of them could be happy together.

Fyodor and Masha were having tea in the garden with Irina. Fyodor had been to the battalion's leaving dinner the previous evening and he was telling the sisters all about it.

'Of course, the Baron and Solyony had their usual quarrel,' said Fyodor. 'The Baron wants them to be friends, but Solyony will not have it.'

Irina looked concerned. 'But why? Surely Solyony can't still be in love with me. That feels like such a long time ago!'

Fyodor shrugged and sipped his tea. 'I could not hear exactly, but

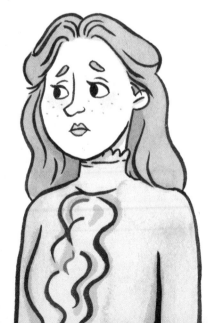

I do believe I heard your name mentioned, dear sister.'

Masha appeared not to be listening. Instead, she kept glancing over to the gate that led out of the house and into town. 'Are you expecting someone, dearest?' asked Fyodor. Masha shook her head.

Then Olga strolled into the garden from the house, Anfisa holding on to her arm. 'Make way for the headmistress!' said Anfisa.

Irina, Masha and Fyodor applauded as their sister took a seat at the tea table.

'Congratulations, Olga,' said Masha. 'We always knew you should be in charge of the school.'

'Now I know who to ask for a pay rise!' Fyodor joked.

Although they were smiling, each sister felt a heaviness in her heart. These would be the last days they

would spend in their family home. Irina was getting married to the Baron the next day and leaving for Moscow. Olga's promotion to headmistress meant that she had her own house nearer the school. She had already asked Anfisa to go with her, fearing that if Anfisa was left in the house with Natasha, she would be fired within minutes. Masha and Fyodor would continue to stay in the town, but Masha would no longer visit her old home. The home they had shared with their parents was not theirs anymore.

Soon after the fire, Andrey had revealed that his gambling debts were so large that he had mortgaged the house. This meant that the house was no longer owned by Andrey and his sisters, but by the bank instead. Andrey was so ashamed of what he had done that he spent most of his time locked away in his study, leaving Natasha to do what she pleased.

However, that afternoon Andrey quietly joined his sisters on the lawn to celebrate Olga's promotion and Irina's marriage.

'Where is Natasha?' asked Fyodor. He was the only one who had noticed that she was missing from the party.

'Inside, looking at wallpaper samples,' replied Andrey. 'She has plans to redecorate the whole house. Although I do not know where she will get the money.'

Olga had never warmed to her sister-in-law. The way Natasha treated Anfisa was not respectable, and she hated how she had redecorated their parents' room.

'I suppose she will start with our room?' Olga asked, bitterly.

Andrey sighed. 'Olga, Irina, Masha,' he said. 'I know Natasha was not your choice of sister-in-law. I know she can be harsh and headstrong. But you must see that, despite all her faults, I love her. I always will.'

Masha reached over the table and squeezed Andrey's hand. She smiled with tears in her eyes. She knew how it felt to love someone unconditionally, no matter what. She felt that way about Alexander.

CHAPTER TWO

After an hour, Anfisa began to clear away the tea things, helped by the sisters. Their afternoon had been almost perfect. Masha had tried to forget that the battalion would be leaving that day, but she could not help keeping her eyes on the gate in case Alexander should call to say goodbye.

As Fyodor balanced a silver tray and followed Anfisa into the house, Alexander finally appeared.

Irina and Olga walked a little way off to sit in the shade of a maple tree. They were giving Alexander and Masha time alone to say goodbye.

Their love had only grown since the fire, and they saw each other every day. Sometimes they talked about what their lives might have been like had they married each other instead. Now Alexander was to move away, and Masha might never see him again.

'I cannot bear it, Alexander,' Masha said, tears rolling down her cheeks. 'How can I go on knowing I will not see you again?'

'You must,' replied Alexander, stroking Masha's hair. 'As must I. I do not have much time. We must say goodbye.'

Alexander and Masha kissed, even though they could be seen by everyone in the house. In that moment, Masha did not care if the whole world found out about their love.

As Alexander gently pushed Masha away to leave, Olga rushed to her sister and caught her as she sank to her knees in despair. The sisters did not notice that Fyodor had joined them. As Alexander left the garden, he did not look back.

'My dear Masha,' Fyodor said, reaching his hand out to his wife. 'My good Masha. I have known for some time that you were happier with Vershinin than with me. But I do not blame you. From this day on I will not mention what has happened today. We can begin again.'

Masha looked up at her husband and blinked away her tears. Most men would have shouted with anger and demanded that their wives leave town, but Fyodor was strong and kind.

'Yes,' she sniffed, taking his hand. 'Yes, Fyodor.' Masha knew that although her husband was not the love of her life, she was the love of his. For now, that would have to be enough.

As Masha steadily rose to her feet, the sisters could hear Natasha's voice drifting from the house. A man with a notepad followed her into the garden, scribbling furiously.

'And this row of maple trees is to be cut down so that I can enjoy the view,' she said, pointing at the trees. 'Have you got all that?'

The man nodded and scuttled away.

'What are you planning?' asked Irina, politely.

Natasha smiled in a self-satisfied way. 'Well, as Olga is to move into the headmistress's house, and you are leaving us tomorrow, I thought I would get ahead with some renovations.'

The sisters looked at each other sadly. Their mother had decorated the house when they moved in.

To them it was perfect. Natasha had been planning her renovation for months now, and with the sisters leaving it was the perfect time to put those plans into action.

'I thought I would move Andrey into your old room,' she said to Olga and Irina. 'I sleep so much better when he is not around. Then I am going to start on the sitting room. Oh, Olga, your clothes …' Natasha looked Olga up and down. Olga was wearing her plain brown teacher's skirt with deep pockets for holding blackboard chalk.

Olga looked down at herself, confused.

'It's fine for *now*,' Natasha continued. 'But maybe next time we have tea you could pick something a little less … dull. Oh well, it's perfect for an unmarried headmistress, I suppose!'

Natasha flashed the sisters a nasty smile and walked happily back into the house.

Chapter Three

Masha wanted nothing more than to go back to the home she shared with Fyodor. The feeling surprised her, but it was a happy kind of surprise. The afternoon had worn her out, and she was furious about Natasha's rude behaviour. She refused to go into her old house to fetch her things, so Fyodor went instead.

As he left, Olga spotted a familiar figure at the gate. It was Doctor Chebutykin.

'My dears! Oh, my dears,' Doctor Chebutykin said, out of breath. He looked as though he had been running. 'I have terrible news.'

'Whatever is the matter?' said Olga, alarmed.

'Do you need some water?' Irina asked.

The doctor steadied himself before he told his story. 'Solyony challenged the Baron to a duel,' he began. Irina placed a hand over her heart.

'He was so angry that the Baron was marrying Irina!'

'When is the duel to take place?' asked Irina, her voice filled with panic.

'It has already happened,' said the doctor. 'The Baron has been killed.'

Irina's head swam. At first, she did not believe the doctor's words. Perhaps he was feeling unwell again, or maybe he had made a mistake? But one look at the doctor's face told her that what he said was true.

'But we were to be married!' cried Irina. She fell into Masha's arms.

'Is this my punishment? I did not love him like I should!'

'You made him happy,' said Masha, stroking her sister's hair and trying to remain calm. 'This was not your fault.'

As the sun started to set behind the maple trees – trees that Natasha would soon cut down – the sisters held on to each other. They knew that it was time to go.

'What happens now?' sniffed Irina.

'We carry on living,' said Masha. 'We are strong. We are sisters. We have each other.'

Olga agreed. 'You can live with me, Irina, and help to teach at the school,' she said. 'Our lives may not be happy now, but we can help the children we teach to be happy.'

Irina nodded. Only a few hours ago she was to be married and to live in Moscow as she had always dreamt. Now that dream was shattered. But if Masha could live without her true love, Irina could get over this and go on living, too.

The sisters held each other's hands and watched the sun disappear in their family's garden one last time.

Strange things are happening in Moscow. A giant cat walks on its hind-legs and a witch with red hair flies through the sky on a broomstick. There's a sell-out show at the theatre with a devilish magician who seems to be behind everything. But how? And what does it have to do with an unfinished book about Jesus and Pontius Pilate?

Can the residents of Moscow figure out what is true, and what is simply a story?